Ellie & the
Sea Monster

VIVIAN FRENCH

Ellie & the Sea Monster

With illustrations by
James de la Rue

Barrington Stoke

For Ewelina, with much love

First published in 2013 in Great Britain by
Barrington Stoke Ltd
18 Walker Street, Edinburgh, EH3 7LP

www.barringtonstoke.co.uk

ISBN: 978-1-78112-270-9

Printed in China by Leo

Contents

Take a ride out past the moon, turn left before you reach the Milky Way, and you'll see Other Earth in front of you.

When you land, take a good look round. Other Earth isn't all that different from the Earth where you live. There are seas and rivers, hills and valleys, mountains and plains, towns and cities.

You may even wonder if you've gone round in a circle, and come back home again.

But don't think about that. Look at the suns. Other Earth has two suns. Oh, and a lot more magic. And wizards. And it's quite a lot smaller than our Earth. And ... no. I'm not going to tell you any more. Read the story and find out for yourself.

Chapter 1

Princess Ellie Has a Plan

Other Earth had lots of kings and queens, and for the most part they got on very well. They visited each other and played tiddlywinks together. Their children met each other at parties – there were a great many children and, of course, they were all princes and princesses. Some of the children went to school, but the rich ones had private tutors.

Princess Ellie was the youngest daughter of the Green King.

"Money and private tutors don't do anyone any good," Princess Ellie told her best friend Princess Pod as they walked home from school one day. "Rich people get so big headed."

Pod nodded. "You're right," she said. "My mum wants me to marry a rich prince. He's called Kittycat, or some stupid name like that. He sounds revolting. He won't even meet me. He sent a rude message saying I wasn't good enough for him. He wants to slay a sea monster, so everyone will think he's a hero, and then find a perfect princess to marry. Huh! Talk about daft! Doesn't he know that it's illegal to hunt sea monsters nowadays?"

"You're better off without him," Ellie said. "Much better off."

"I know." Pod kicked at a pebble. "Has your mum got any plans for you?" she asked.

Ellie shook her head. "No. My eleven sisters have worn her out. Twelve princesses are an awful lot to think about. And I told her I wanted to seek my fortune before I bothered with any of that prince stuff." She gave Pod a sly look. "Can you keep a secret?"

Pod looked surprised. "You know I can. I'm your best friend, aren't I?"

"Yes. Sorry." Ellie patted her friend on the back. "Listen … you know the Second Sun is going to set at the end of the month?"

"As if I could forget." Pod looked gloomy. "We've been doing Second Sun projects for weeks and weeks and weeks at school." She screwed up her face and imitated her teacher. "Princess Pod, I want you to write out 100 times in your best writing, 'A human life is short with all its cares – the second sun sets every thousand years!'"

Ellie giggled.

Pod sighed. "I hate Mr Gluefrog," she said. "It took me ages to write all those lines out."

"Well, that's your fault," Ellie told her. "You told him the Second Sun sets every 20 months!"

4

Pod did her best to look dignified. "Anyone can make a mistake."

"Well ..." Ellie pulled her friend closer. "Do you remember what Mr Gluefrog said about the Hill of Promises?"

Pod's eyes opened wide. "Oh no ... oh, Ellie! You didn't believe him? All that stuff about wishes?"

Ellie nodded. "Why shouldn't it be true? It's got to be worth a try!" Now it was her turn to imitate Mr Gluefrog. "'If you stand high upon the Hill of Promises as the Second Sun goes down, then a wish will be yours to keep.' Oh, Pod! It has to be worth trying! Just think – a wish!"

"What will you wish for?" Pod asked.

"I don't know." Ellie's eyes shone. "But I really want a wish. I have this feeling I'll know just what to wish for when I get it. I'm going to find the Hill, and I'll see what happens. And, Pod – guess what? I'm going tonight!"

Pod stopped dead and stared at Ellie. "Tonight?"

Ellie nodded. "I've got it all planned. Half-term starts today, so I've got a week. If I can get to the other side of the Abominable Sea by tomorrow evening, I'll have loads of time. The end of the month isn't till Monday. I'll be sitting on the top of the Hill of Promises well before then. There'll be plenty of time for me to get back before school starts again. And I'll have my wish – my very own beautiful, sparkly wish!"

Pod still didn't look too sure. "What will your mum say?" she asked. "Aren't your family having a huge party for the setting of the Second Sun? Mine are."

"Yes, they're planning a massive beanfeast," Ellie said. "But that's why they won't miss me! Mum will be much too busy worrying about cakes and presents and fireworks and so on. And she's hoping my sister Rosetta will propose to Prince Biscuit the Second. They'll never notice I'm gone, just as long as I'm back by the end of the week."

Pod sighed. "You are lucky. I'd come with you, but my mum would have a fit."

"I'll tell you what," said Ellie. "I'll try to keep my wish till I get back. Then you can help me choose what to wish for."

"Oh, Ellie!" Pod beamed. "You're the best friend ever!"

"Can I tell Rosetta I'm staying with you?" Ellie asked. "Just in case Mum asks? I'm sure she won't, but you never know."

"Sure thing," said Pod.

Chapter 2

Pimple Barks and Bounces

———————

It was after ten when Ellie sneaked out of the Green Palace on tip-toes. Her eleven sisters had taken ages going to bed. Rosetta and Hollissa had had an argument that had rumbled on for hours.

"Sisters!" Ellie muttered to herself as she ran down the path. "Maybe I should use my wish to wish that I was an only child!"

A moment later, she shook her head. "Nah! That would be a terrible waste of a wish. Besides, my sisters are OK most of the time. If it weren't for my sisters I'd never get to go on adventures by myself." She stopped and checked her bag. "Now, have I got everything I

need? String ... peppermints ... spare jumper ...
socks ... and five gold coins. Yup! That should
do just fine." She swung her bag onto her back
and jogged off.

"Yip yip yip yip yip!"

Ellie swung round. "Pimple?"

A small black-and-white dog hurled himself
at her. He was barking like mad and trying to
lick her knees.

"Pimple!" Ellie stared at the little dog
in surprise. "I thought I'd shut you in with
Rosetta. You're a bad, bad dog to follow me!"

Even to her own ears Ellie didn't sound very
angry. Pimple went on barking and bouncing
up and down.

Ellie sighed. "Oh, well. You may as well
come too." She bent down and scratched
Pimple's ears. "To tell the truth, I'm really

pleased to see you. I was beginning to feel lonely. We'll take the short cut through the Midnight Forest – but it's very dark and scary. Mind you do as you're told!"

"Yip!" barked Pimple. He trotted along next to Ellie as she left the path and headed towards the forest of tall and creaky pine trees.

The Midnight Forest was pitch black. It was impossible to see anything. Ellie stopped walking after she had scraped her knees twice and banged her head three times. She was still only at the very edge of the forest.

Ellie sighed as she rubbed her head. "Why didn't I bring a torch?" she asked Pimple. Pimple sat down beside her and panted hard. Ellie leaned against a tree trunk and had a think.

"I reckon," she said at last, "we'll have to take the path that goes round the forest.

We're never going to get through these trees. The ferry leaves from the Unexpected Cliffs tomorrow morning. If we run all the way, we might make it."

"Yip," barked Pimple.

Ellie bent down to pat him. "Good dog," she said. "Let's get going." And they both began to run ...

Ellie and Pimple collapsed on the ground just as the moon sank down until it was level with the Second Sun. The sky was a mix of green and gold, and the wind had begun to blow the night clouds away.

"We can only rest for a minute!" Ellie panted. "It will be morning soon. We can sleep on the ferry. Let's go!"

Ellie struggled to her feet and ran on down the path. Pimple bounced along behind her. All night long the Midnight Forest had loomed on one side, and on the other side were the fields and hedges of the Green Kingdom. Now, at last, these gave way to sandy dunes and low rocks. There was a smell of salt in the air. Sea birds wheeled and shrieked above Ellie as she and Pimple rushed on.

"We must be nearly there," Ellie puffed. "Look out for the cliffs, Pimple. There aren't any warning signs. Dad said he once nearly fell – aaaaagh!!"

And with a loud yell, Princess Ellie fell over the edge of the Unexpected Cliffs. Pimple hovered for a moment and then launched himself after her.

WHEEEE … THUMP!!

Princess Ellie and Pimple landed on something soft, squelchy and damp.

"Ooooh," said the something and burst into tears. "Boo hoo! Boo hoo hooo! Boo hoo hooo!"

Chapter 3

A Remarkably Handsome Prince

Ellie sat up and looked round. "Goodness!" she said. "What a very strange seashore!"

Ellie was right. Instead of rocks, the sand was covered with strange rubbery purple lumps and bumps. Every purple lump had a wide-open mouth, and every purple lump was sobbing and wailing.

"Oops!" Ellie said, as she got to her feet. "I'm so sorry to have landed on you like this. I do hope I haven't hurt you."

"Of course you haven't," said a voice. "They're the Blubbering Rocks. They always cry. Don't you know anything?"

Ellie span round and saw a monster. A scaly, bug-eyed, blue-green, big-nosed sea monster. A sea monster that was sitting on a stone with his arms folded. It was looking at Ellie as if she was very silly indeed.

"Yarooo!" Pimple howled. "Yaroooo!" He tried to hide behind Ellie's legs.

Ellie picked him up. "It's OK, Pimple," she said. "It's only a sea monster."

The sea monster snorted loudly. "I beg your pardon. Did I hear you call me a ... a monster?"

Ellie looked at it in surprise. "Well ... Yes, I did. I mean, you are a monster, aren't you?"

The sea monster sat bolt upright and glared at Ellie.

"I am certainly NOT a monster," he said. "I mean, do I sound like a monster? If you saw me in my – er – normal state you would see at

16

once that I'm a prince. In fact, people tell me that I'm a remarkably handsome prince." He snorted again, and his lip curled. "On the other hand, you appear to be a remarkably plain princess, my dear."

Ellie stared at the monster. He did look like a sea monster. He was covered in scales and his skin was a greenish blue colour. He smelled like a sea monster too – a strong whiff of old wet seaweed hung all around him. What's more, he was sitting in a place where real and proper sea monsters might be found. But it was true that he didn't sound quite right. The sea monsters that Ellie had met before had all just grunted. Or gurgled. Or burped.

"You don't look much like a remarkably handsome prince," Ellie said. "What happened to you?"

The sea monster paused. "There was an – erm – how shall I put it? A nasty scene. With a wizard, if you must know. But I'll soon be back to my usual self. I'm off to the Hill of Promises on the Hopeful Islands. I know a secret about the setting of the Second Sun, you see."

"Oh." Why did the sea monster have to have the same plans as her? Ellie wasn't sure that she wanted company on her travels. Particularly not company that seemed to think so much of himself. But she did need advice. "That's where we're going," she said. "Do you know what time the ferry leaves?"

"Ferry? What ferry?" The sea monster stared at her.

"The ferry to the Hopeful Islands," Ellie said.

The sea monster went on staring. "There isn't a ferry. There's a turtle. It's due any minute now."

"A turtle?" Now it was Ellie's turn to stare.

"Didn't you check any of your travel plans?"
The sea monster rolled his piggy little eyes.
"There's a Turtle Express here. It takes you
directly to the Hopeful Islands. Mind you, there
may not be room. I was here before you, and
I'll be travelling first class."

Ellie shrugged. "I don't see any queues.
Only me and Pimple and you." She looked at
the sea monster's large and wobbly body. "Um.
How big is this turtle?"

"See for yourself," said the monster. "Look!
Here it comes."

Chapter 4

All Aboard the Turtle Express

Ellie looked out to sea. A massive ripple was coming closer and closer. Then the wrinkly head and shiny shell of a huge turtle rose above the waves. It came swimming towards Ellie and Pimple and the sea monster. The turtle reached the shore and heaved itself onto the sand.

"All aboard for the Hopeful Islands," it called. It had a voice like gravel. "And hurry up. I want to be back in time for my breakfast."

"Ahem. I wish to travel first class," the sea monster said as he waddled forwards.

The turtle inspected him.

"If I'm not much mistaken," it said, "you're a sea monster. And I don't take sea monsters. You can swim, can't you? Don't be so blooming lazy."

The sea monster looked astonished. "I'm not a sea monster," he said. "I'm a prince! This is only a – how shall I put it? A short-term arrangement."

"Oh yeah?" The turtle did not look impressed. "Well, what I say is, I don't take sea monsters, no matter how short or long the arrangement." The turtle turned to Ellie with a sweet smile. "You and that little doggy of yours – you hop on. I'll have you there in no time, a skinny little thing like you."

"But – I say – wait!" The sea monster waved his arms wildly. Ellie thought he sounded very scared all of a sudden. "I've simply GOT to get to the Hill of Promises before the Second Sun sets. If I don't – oh, I can't bear to think about it!"

"Swim," said the turtle. "It'll do you good." Then the turtle turned its huge body round. Ellie held Pimple tight and climbed carefully onto the turtle's shell.

"PLEASE!" said the sea monster, and his voice wobbled. "You – Princess with a dog – you ask the turtle. I can't stay like this for ever! I can't!" He stretched out his scaly arms to Ellie and a slow tear dribbled down his large green nose.

Ellie sighed. She didn't much like the sea monster, but she couldn't help feeling sorry for him. It was clear he was desperate.

"Maybe the turtle could give you a tow," she suggested. "Would that be all right, Mr – er – Mrs –" Ellie stopped. She had no idea if the turtle was male or female.

The turtle let out a deep chuckle. "Mrs Turtle, that's me," she said. "OK, then. He can hang on to my tail. But if he lets go – too bad. Lazy things, sea monsters. I'm not going back for him."

"Thank you very much," Ellie said. She glared at the sea monster. "Go on. Say thank you."

The monster still looked worried. "Oh. Of course. Thanks." He waded into the water. Ellie was surprised to see him shiver.

'That's odd,' she thought. 'Very odd. Could he really be a prince?' She shook her head. It didn't seem very likely ...

The turtle trundled deep into the waves. The sea monster took a firm grip on her tail. Ellie sat high up on the shell with Pimple on her lap. She was pleased to find two leather straps to hold on to, as the turtle was swaying in a scary way.

Behind Ellie, the sea monster began to moan. He sounded terrified. Ellie saw that he had his eyes shut tight as he hung on to Mrs Turtle's large and leathery tail.

A shred of doubt flickered in Ellie's mind. It was true that he wasn't behaving like the usual kind of sea monster. And wizards were tricky things if you upset them ... but surely not that tricky. You'd have to do something really dreadful to be changed into a sea monster. Really really dreadful ... 'Would a prince ever be that bad?' Ellie wondered.

Mrs Turtle swayed in the waves and Ellie gave up on the puzzle. She concentrated instead on hanging on to Mrs Turtle's leather straps. Far behind them in the distance, the Blubbering Rocks wailed and cried.

Chapter 5

The Sea Monster Learns a Lesson

———————

"Here we are," Mrs Turtle said cheerfully. "Everybody off."

Ellie rubbed her eyes. A huge cliff face towered above her, and the First and Second Suns were high in the sky. The sea monster was stretched out in a heap on the pebbly beach. He wasn't moving.

'I must have been dozing,' Ellie thought as she slid off the turtle's back.

Pimple leapt in front of her with a loud "Yip! Yip! Yip!" of joy. The sea monster groaned and lifted his head.

"What day is it?" he asked.

"Saturday," Ellie said. "Well – I think it is."

"Monday," said Mrs Turtle. "We are in a different time zone here."

"MONDAY?" Ellie and the sea monster shouted as they stared at her in horror.

Mrs Turtle made a tut-tut noise. "Don't they teach you anything in school these days?" she asked. "You lose two days when you cross the Abominable Sea. Start on a Saturday and it's a Monday when you get across. On the other hand, you'll gain two days when you travel back. Travel on a Tuesday and you'll arrive on the Sunday before. You'll be back before you started, if you're fast enough. Understand?"

No. Ellie and the sea monster didn't understand.

Mrs Turtle looked at their goggly eyes and open mouths.

28

"Aha!" she said. "I see. You two are hoping to get to the Hill of Promises to find a wish!" She squinted up at the two suns in the sky overhead. "Well – you could do it. If you hurry." She gave the sea monster a sour glance, and turned to Ellie.

"I'd leave THAT behind if I were you, duckie," she whispered. "Sea monsters aren't made for speed. You hop along on your own. Best way is up those cliffs, across the Twisting River and then up that hill as fast as you can." She nodded her wrinkly head. "The very best of luck to you, my dear."

With a wave of her flipper, the turtle dived into the sea. Ellie saw a flick of her tail and then she was gone.

The sea monster burst into noisy tears.

Ellie felt like crying herself, but it didn't seem the right moment. She looked at the cliffs, then started to walk towards them.

"Don't go without me!" The sea monster was on his feet, blowing his nose with a noise like a trumpet. "Please don't go without me!"

A battle was going on inside Ellie's head. She wanted her wish. She wanted her wish very badly. She had always dreamed of having a wish of her very own. And now, if she waited for the sea monster, she might miss the chance for ever and ever and ever.

On the other hand, the sea monster needed a wish far more than she did ... if he really was a prince. But was he? Could he be? Was he telling the truth?

Ellie turned to the sea monster. "OK," she said. "I want to know the truth. You say you're a prince. Prove it!"

The sea monster blinked. A trail of silvery snot dribbled down his chin.

"I am!" he said. "I know I am! It was Wizard Bluegrim. He put a spell on me. He said I behaved like a monster. He said he would teach me a lesson and make me a real monster until I did something to show I had learned my lesson. Wizard Bluegrim waved his arms and there was a horrible smell of seaweed. Then BANG!!! I was covered with disgusting scales."

"Hmm," said Ellie. "I've heard of Bluegrim. But I'm still not sure I believe you're a prince. You could be anyone. What's your name?"

The sea monster drooped. "That's the worst of it. I can't remember. My mind is all foggy. I can't even remember where I come from ... I've been making it up as I go along ever since I set out on this journey. But I do know that I've got to get a wish. Then I can be myself again."

Ellie rubbed her nose. "But when we met, you told me you'd made all your travel plans ..."

The sea monster shuffled a bit, looking ashamed. "I was trying to be clever. I'd seen the turtle swimming towards us from the top of the Unexpected Cliffs."

"OK," Ellie said. "We'll go together. But you've got to go fast – as fast as you can."

And she swung herself onto the first rock at the bottom of the cliffs.

Ellie, Pimple and the sea monster struggled upwards inch by inch. It was hard work. The sea monster complained all the way.

"It's so STEEP!" he wailed. "My feet HURT! And I'm so TIRED!"

Ellie folded her arms and glared at him.

"If you don't stop moaning," she said, "we'll never get to the Hill of Promises. And if we don't get to the Hill of Promises before the Second Sun goes down, you won't get your wish.

And if you don't get your wish, then you'll never ever change back into ... into ... whatever it was you were before you were a sea monster."

The sea monster began to snuffle. "You're so mean to me," he said. "I told you ... I'm a prince. A remarkably handsome prince." He wiped his dribbly nose with his scaly paw and sniffed. "The prettiest princesses were crazy about me before I had my little ... er ... accident." He gave Ellie a sour look. "You wouldn't have stood a chance."

Ellie thought about slapping him. Then she changed her mind and decided to be kind. He was tired. She got snappy too when she was tired.

In fact, now she came to think about it, she was tired. Very tired indeed.

"OK," Ellie said. "If that's the way you feel about me, I'll go on by myself."

"NO!" The sea monster pretended to smile at Ellie. "I take it back! I do! You're wonderful! I'm sure that one day you'll meet a prince who likes plain princesses. He won't even notice that you haven't got big blue eyes and golden curls, and you'll live happily ever after!"

Ellie took a deep breath. She counted to ten, then counted another five.

"Listen," she said. She kept her voice as calm as she could. "Listen to me. You really ARE a monster. You're the worst sort there is. You're a monster on the inside, not just on the outside. Haven't you ever noticed that it's the way people behave that matters? Not what they look like? Now, I'm sorry, but I've had enough. You get to the Hill of Promises if you can. Pimple and I are going to collect our wish. Good luck – and goodbye."

Chapter 6

Where Is Pimple?

Ellie stormed up to the top of the cliff in a burst of fury.

A huge silence hung in the air behind her.

The Twisting River was at the top of the cliffs, as the turtle had said. It was wide, but not deep. Ellie plunged in. She half waded, half swam across. She was still feeling hot and bothered, and she was grateful for the cool blue water. She splashed out on the other side and whistled for Pimple.

No Pimple came.

Ellie's stomach lurched.

"Pimple!" she called. "Pimple? Here! Good dog!"

There was no answer. No bark. No flurry of flying feet. Ellie whistled and whistled until her lips were sore, but still Pimple did not come.

Ellie's mind was racing. When was the last time she had seen Pimple? She was sure that he had scrambled up to the top of the cliff with her. She was almost sure that he had been at her side when she came to the river bank ... or had he? Her mind had been so full of the sea monster's stupid remarks that she hadn't been thinking about anything else.

"It's all that horrid monster's fault," Ellie muttered. But then she shook her head. "No. That's not fair. It's my fault. I should have been looking out for him. He's only a little dog. Oh, Pimple! Dear Pimple – where are you?"

And Ellie began to wade back across the river, whistling and calling, and calling and whistling.

It was much harder going back. The current pulled at Ellie's legs. It pushed her and twisted her towards the bank. Ellie kicked and struggled and paddled with her hands, but in the end she was forced to give up. She sat down at the water's edge and wiped the tears from her eyes.

Then Ellie had a thought. Could Pimple be with the sea monster? It didn't seem very likely – but it was better than no hope at all. Ellie stood up and stared across the river.

Yes! There was the sea monster. He had reached the top of the cliff and now he was lumbering towards the bank ... but he was on his own.

Ellie sat down to wait. Even if Pimple wasn't with him, the sea monster might have seen him.

"Are you waiting for me?" The sea monster sounded hopeful as he surged out of the river, water streaming from his sides. "How are we doing for time? The Second Sun doesn't look that low yet. What do you think?"

Ellie had almost forgotten about the Second Sun. She gave it a quick glance. It was low in the sky, but the sea monster was right. It would be a little while yet before it set …

"Oh!" Ellie shouted. "Of course!"

"What? What is it?" the sea monster asked. "Haven't we got enough time?"

"No – it's Pimple!"

The monster looked blank. Ellie realised he had no idea what she was talking about.

"My dog. He's called Pimple!" Ellie said. "I've lost him, but I've had a brilliant idea! I can use my wish. I can wish him back here with me!"

The sea monster sank to the ground in a flubbery heap.

"You'd use your wish to get your dog back?" he asked Ellie. He sounded as if he didn't believe her.

"Yes! Of course! I couldn't bear to lose him." Ellie was feeling so much better that she didn't notice the astonishment on the sea monster's face.

"But ... I mean ... couldn't you get another dog when you get back home?" the sea monster asked.

Ellie took a deep breath. She started to count to ten, but then she noticed the look on the sea monster's face. He didn't mean to be annoying. He was making a serious suggestion.

"No," Ellie said. "No, I couldn't. You don't understand, do you? Pimple's not just any old dog – he's my dog. It's like – it's like my sisters.

If something happened to one of them, I couldn't go and get a new one, could I? It would never be the same."

"Oh," the sea monster said. He screwed up his nose. "I think I see." He gave Ellie an odd little sideways look. "I don't have any sisters. Or brothers. Or a dog," he said.

Ellie nodded. "I guessed as much." Then she thought about what she had said. "You know what?" she asked. "I think I believe you. You really are a prince under a spell."

"Yes," said the sea monster. To Ellie's surprise, his voice was humble. "Yes, I am. And – er – I'm sorry about Pimple."

Ellie's eyes opened wide. For once she couldn't think of anything to say.

"Oh. Um. Thanks," she said at last. Then she shook her head. "Hey! We'd better get going or neither of us will get our wish!"

Chapter 7

Can Wishes Come True?

Ellie and the sea monster climbed the Hill of Promises in silence. The Second Sun was floating down and down. The clouds in the west were turning pink, purple and deepest indigo. They began to run as they reached the top. As they stood there panting, a shining ray of sunlight shot across the sky and turned the grass around them into liquid gold.

"Hurry up!" said Ellie. "Ask for your wish!"

The sea monster went pale. Well ... pale blue and pale green. He shut his eyes.

"Please!" he whispered. "Please! Make me my old self again!"

Nothing happened.

The sea monster opened his eyes and collapsed.

Ellie bent over him. "Are you OK?"

"No," the sea monster whispered. "No ..." He clutched at Ellie's hand. "Please. PLEASE?"

Ellie knew at once what he wanted. Her head spun and she trembled all over. The ray of sunlight was growing fainter ...

Ellie crouched down beside the sea monster. "OK," she said. "But if I use my wish for you, you have to use yours for me. You have to wish for Pimple. Promise?"

The sea monster nodded.

"I wish," Ellie said loudly and clearly. "I wish for the sea monster to be changed back into his real self."

The rush of wind nearly knocked Ellie off her feet. She twirled round and staggered against an arm. The arm grabbed her and steadied her.

"Watch out," said the remarkably handsome prince standing beside her. "You nearly knocked us both over!"

"Hurry!" said Ellie. "Hurry! Wish for Pimple!"

"No way," said the prince. "I've got a much better idea!" He shut his eyes with their long dark curly eyelashes and ...

The wind whirled Ellie and the prince through the air as the Second Sun set at last. They whirled over the river, across the sea and down, down, down towards the Green Kingdom. As she flew, Ellie felt angrier than she had ever felt in her entire life.

'I'll kill him,' Ellie thought. 'I hate him! How could he? He's the most horrible beastly nasty disgusting person that I've ever met in my life ... Even being a sea monster was much too good for him ..."

Ellie and the prince landed with a soft thump. At once Ellie flung herself at the prince, spitting and yelling and shouting, her fists flying.

"HEY!" he said, as best he could. "Stop! STOP! Look!"

Ellie didn't want to stop – but then she heard a noise that made her freeze.

"Yip yip yip yip YIP!"

"PIMPLE!" she shrieked.

Pimple dashed towards Ellie. His tail was wagging so fast it was a miracle that he didn't take off. He and Ellie met half way, and the

next minute they were cuddling and hugging as
if they would never stop.

"There," said the prince. "Better?"

Ellie looked up from kissing Pimple's ears. "Oh, thank you," she said. "Thank you a million million times. But ... what did you wish for?"

"Well ..." the prince said. "I wished for a happy ending." He leaned down and patted Pimple. "But I wished for the happy ending that you would want. Not me."

Ellie picked up Pimple and got to her feet. She felt a bit wobbly.

"Wow," she said. "WOW! I have to admit – that was clever."

The prince looked embarrassed. "Thanks."

"By the way," Ellie said. "What's your name? Have you remembered?"

The prince cleared his throat. "Erm. It's Kitterkat. Prince Kitterkat. Your friend

Princess Pod might have mentioned me. I was – I was just a bit rude about her."

He cleared his throat again. "No. Correct that. I was very rude. In fact, I was very rude indeed. I was so rude I upset her uncle. It turned out he was a wizard. Wizard Bluegrim."

"Oh!" said Ellie. "I remember! Pod told me you didn't want to meet her. You said you were going to kill a sea monster and become a hero and hunt for the perfect princess!"

Prince Kitterkat looked even more embarrassed. "Yes. And then look what happened to me!"

"Hmm," said Ellie. "Well, you must admit you deserved it. Pod's lovely! She is a perfect princess. You'll never find anyone more perfect."

Prince Kitterkat swallowed hard.

"You may be right," the prince said. "Erm. It's just that ... it's just ... erm. In fact, I'd say you were more perfect. A lot more perfect. And a lot more lovely too. Erm. Excuse me. I think I'd better go home now."

Prince Kitterkat gave Pimple one last pat, then ran down the path as if hundreds of wizards were after him.

Ellie watched him go with a smile.

"Fancy that," she said. "I think he actually likes me! But never mind that now. I've got a bone to pick with Pod. How dare she not tell me that her uncle's a wizard?"

And Ellie and Pimple went hurrying along the path that led to the castle where Princess Pod and her family lived.

Half way along the path Ellie gave another happy skip.

"Guess what, Pimple!" she said. "I've just thought of something else! It must still be Sunday back here! We're going to be in time for the Second Sunset party after all!"

Our books are tested
for children and young people by
children and young people.

Thanks to everyone who consulted on
a manuscript for their time and effort in
helping us to make our books better
for our readers.

More from *Barrington Stoke...*

Sweetness and Lies
KAREN MCCOMBIE

New girl Amber is a champion ice-skater who can get free passes for Alton Towers and goes to see her granny in Barbados in the holidays. It's almost too good to be true.

Tilly's friend Mia reckons Amber is a total liar. And Tilly and Mia are best friends, so Tilly has to trust Mia. Right?

The Cupcake Wedding
GILLIAN CROSS

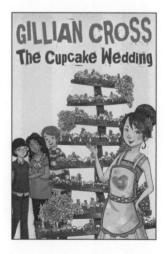

Holly's sister Mia is going to marry her boyfriend James. But they're only 18. Are they too young to be married?

Soon all of Holly's friends and family have agreed to help out with the wedding. But Holly has her work cut out for her when the bride and groom both get cold feet!

Cherry Green, Story Queen
ANNIE DALTON

Mia wishes she could leave the foster home. Be back at home with her mum. But that's impossible. Mia knows she just has to learn to live with it. Like Billy, Juno and Kyle.

But then Cherry Green arrives with a spring in her step and a book in her bag. Can she help them find the happy ending they all need?

The Genie
MARY HOOPER

It was supposed to be a present for Fudge's dad. A little box from a jumble sale.

No way was there supposed to be a Genie inside. A Genie who promises he can make all Fudge's wishes come true. Which does sound pretty cool.

But Fudge is about to find out that you have to be very careful what you wish for!

www.barringtonstoke.co.uk